To ......Ainsley...............................

For being good.
Merry Christmas!
From **Santa**

Almely

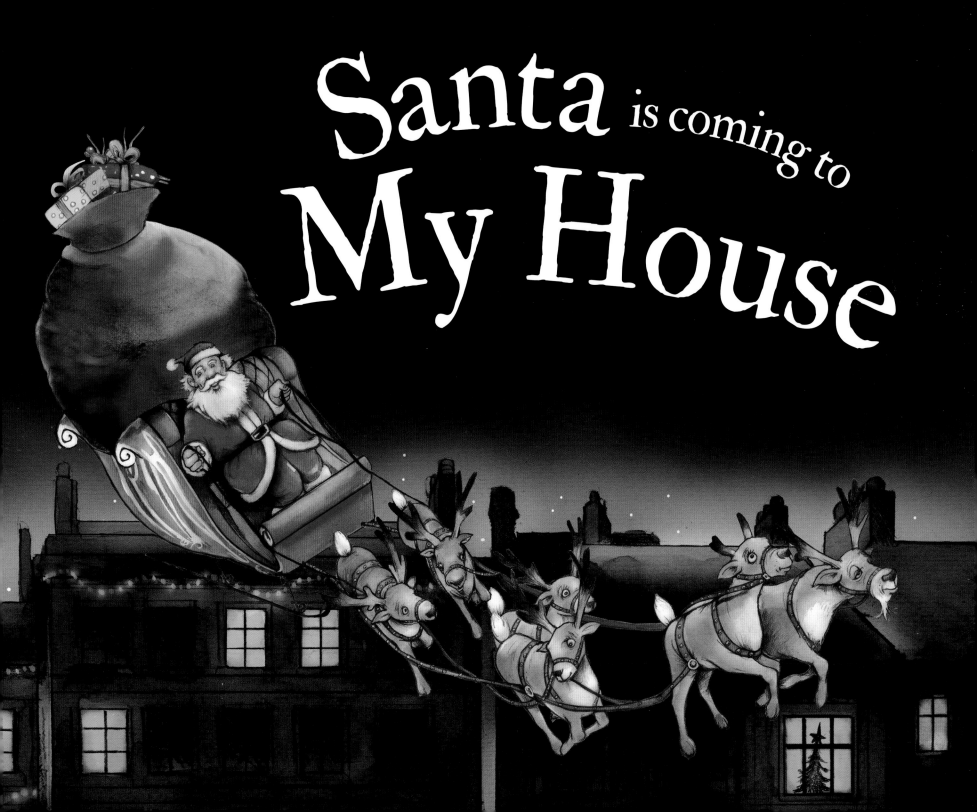

Santa is coming to My House

Written by Steve Smallman
Illustrated by Robert Dunn

Copyright © Hometown World Ltd. 2019

Published by Sourcebooks Jabberwocky,
an imprint of Sourcebooks, Inc.
P.O. Box 4410, Naperville, Illinois 60567-4410
(630) 961-3900
jabberwockykids.com

Date of Production: May 2019
Run Number: 5014816
Printed and bound in China (1010)
10 9 8 7 6 5 4 3 2 1

Santa is coming to My House

Written by Steve Smallman
Illustrated by Robert Dunn

sourcebooks
jabberwocky

"Well?"

boomed Santa. "Have all the children been good this year?"

"Well...uh...mostly," answered the little old elf, as he bustled across the busy workshop to Santa's desk.

Santa peered down at the elf from behind the tall, teetering piles of letters that the children had sent him.

"Mostly?" asked Santa, looking over the top of his glasses.

"Yes...but they've all been especially good in the last few days!" said the elf.

"Jolly good!" chuckled Santa.

"Then we'd better get their presents loaded up!"

Even though the sack of presents was

really, really big

and the elves were really, really small,

they seemed to have no trouble loading it onto Santa's sleigh.
Though how they managed to fit such a big sack onto one little sleigh
even they didn't know. But somehow they did.

"Splendid!" boomed Santa. "We're ready to go!"

"Er...not quite, Santa," said the little old elf. "One of our reindeer is missing!"

"Missing?

Which reindeer is missing?" asked Santa.

"The youngest one, Santa," said the elf. "It's his first flight tonight. I've called him and called him, but..."

Just then, a young reindeer strolled up, munching on a large carrot.

"Where have you been?"

asked Santa.

But the youngest reindeer was crunching so loudly that it was no wonder he hadn't heard the little old elf calling.

"Oh well, never mind," said Santa, giving the reindeer a little wink. He took out his Santa-nav and tapped in the coordinates for the first town he was visiting. "This will guide us there in no time."

CRUNCH!
CRUNCH!
CRUNCH!

With a flick of the reins and a jerk of the harness, off they went, racing through the sky.

"Ho, ho, ho!"

laughed Santa.

"We'll soon have all these presents delivered!"

Santa's sleigh flew through the starry night, heading south across the Arctic Ocean. On they flew in the wintry air, crossing the coast. In the wink of an eye, the sleigh was flying above mountains and plains, cities and towns. The youngest reindeer was very excited. He had never been away from the North Pole before.

They were nearing their destination
when, suddenly, they ran into a blizzard.
Snowflakes whirled around the sleigh.

They couldn't see a thing!

The youngest reindeer was getting a bit worried,
but Santa didn't seem concerned.

"In two miles..."

said the Santa-nav in a bossy lady's voice,

"...keep left at the next star."

"But, ma'am," Santa blustered, "I can't see any stars in all this snow!"
Soon they were

hopelessly lost!

Ding-dong!
Ding-dong!

Then, through the howling blizzard, the youngest reindeer heard a faint, ringing sound.

Ding-dong!

He looked over at the old reindeer with the red nose. But he had his head down.

(Red nose...I wonder who that could be?)

Ding-dong!
Ding-dong!

Ding-dong!
Ding-dong!

There was that sound again, like church bells ringing. The youngest reindeer turned around to look at Santa. But Santa wasn't listening. He seemed to be arguing with a little box with buttons on it.

With a flick of the harness and a jerk of the reins, the youngest reindeer gave a sharp **TUG** and headed off toward the sound of the bells, pulling Santa and his sleigh behind him!

"Whoa!"

cried Santa, pulling his hat straight.
"What's going on?" Then, to his
surprise, he heard the ringing sound.

"Well done, young reindeer!" he shouted cheerfully.
"It must be church bells. Don't worry, children,
Santa is coming!"

Then, suddenly...

CRUNCH!

The sleigh hit something as it plummeted through the snow clouds.
"You have arrived!"
said the Santa-nav unhelpfully.

Finally, when the snow had died down and the clouds parted, Santa discovered exactly where they were...

...stuck, right at the very top of the town Christmas tree!

"Everybody, PULL!"

The reindeer **PULLED** with all their might until,
at last, with a screeching noise, the sleigh scraped
clear of the Christmas tree and Santa steered them
safely over the town hall, past the library,
and down into the park.

Luckily, there
was no real
damage done, but
the packages had all
been jumbled up. Santa
quickly sorted out the
presents into order again.

"All right," said Santa. "Thanks
to this young reindeer I know where
we are now. Don't worry, children,

Santa is coming!"

Santa drove his sleigh expertly from
rooftop to rooftop all over town,
popping in and out of chimneys
as fast as he could go.

(Which was
pretty fast
for a chubby
fellow!)

There were big chimneys and small chimneys,
tall chimneys and short chimneys. He squeezed down
thin chimneys and plummeted down fat chimneys.

The youngest reindeer was
amazed at how quickly they went.
Santa never seemed to get tired at all!
And it looked like all the children
were going to be very lucky this year!
But the youngest reindeer was
starting to feel a bit weary
and quite hungry, too!

In house after house, Santa delved inside his sack for packages of every shape and size.

He piled them under the Christmas trees and carefully filled up the stockings with surprises.

Santa took a little bite out of each cookie,
a tiny sip of milk, wiped his beard,
and popped the carrots into his sack.

In house after house, the good
children had left out a large plate
of cookies, a small glass of milk,
and a big, crunchy carrot.

From north to south, from east to west, along the main streets, through the side streets, and ALL the places in between, Santa and his sleigh visited every house in town.

Santa delivered presents to Andrew, Alison,
Anna, Arabella, Archie, Ashley...the list
went on and on!...Zac, Zara, Zeb, Zoe, Zybil.

(Zybil? That must be a
spelling mistake, surely!)

SUPERMARKET

Finally, Santa had delivered the last present on his long list.

"Great moons and stars!" sighed Santa. "It's past midnight and my sack seems as heavy as ever! I hope I haven't forgotten anyone."

Santa opened his sack to check...but it was full of juicy, crunchy carrots!

Santa divided the carrots among all the reindeer.
"Well done!" he said, patting the youngest reindeer gently on the nose.

But the youngest reindeer didn't hear him...he was too busy munching!

Then it was time to set off for home. Santa reset his Santa-nav once more
to the North Pole, and soon they were speeding over the homes of the
sleeping children through the crisp, starry night.

"Ho, ho, ho!"
laughed Santa.

"Merry Christmas,
Everyone!"